Tales in Rhyme
Aladdin
and the Magic Lamp

Sia Gupta

Om
KIDZ
An imprint of Om Books International

Aladdin
and the Magic Lamp

I will tell you a tale in rhyme,

That once upon a time

There was a poor, orphan boy in town,

He always had a smile, never a frown!

Aladdin was his simple and unique name,

His dream was lots of money and fame.

A monkey named Abu was his only friend,

Though Abu's thieving ways, he tried to mend.

Everybody knew Aladdin was a thief,

To live, he had to steal, was his belief.

Aladdin was actually a very generous boy,

He would share his food to give others joy.

Everyday, at the palace, he would gaze,
And think, *It must be nice to just sit and laze.*
While in the palace Princess Jasmine thought
About being a common villager, a lot.

She had to follow an old tradition.
Marrying a prince was her mission.
'I will marry only if I fall in love,' she said,
'Even if the land is left without any head.'

She had a ferocious Bengal tiger for a pet.
He saved her from any worry or threat.
Rajah was his majestic name,
From India, as a cub, he came.

One day, Jasmine decided to run away
To escape; to God, she really did pray.
She escaped in disguise that night,
Into the town, looking merry and bright.

In the town, she saw a poor, helpless boy.

From a shop, she handed him a small toy.

As the shopkeeper shouted, Aladdin appeared,

And together they both ran and disappeared.

He fell in love with her at first sight;

To him, she was everything good and bright.

He gave Jasmine a handsome smile,

And they stared at each other for a while.

Meanwhile, the king, who could have been wiser,

Discussed with Jafar, his royal, intelligent advisor,

About how the princess did not agree to marry,

The age-old tradition, she refused to carry.

The cunning advisor wanted the kingdom.

He wanted to cloud the king's wisdom,

But for that he needed a magical thing,

Which, from the Cave of Doom he had to bring.

He called his parrot and his private servant,

And off to the mysterious cave they went.

The servant went to look for the lamp

Into the cave so cold, dark and damp.

The cave had a wall of joining rocks that broke;

Then in a frightening tone, the mighty boulder spoke,

'Only worthy Aladdin can come into the depths inside.

None other can be here, though many have tried.'

The next day, Jafar called his soldiers to ask
To capture Aladdin, was their important task.
So they broke into Aladdin's shack,
And waited for Aladdin to return back.

The palace guards caught him there,
And tried to drag him to Jafar's lair.
Jasmine stood up and removed her disguise,
She was the princess, they soon did realise!

She ordered, 'Stop! leave him alone.'
She commanded in her royal tone.
The guards had orders from Jafar himself.
She would have to go and ask him herself.

Jasmine ran into the palace to find the king;
Ready to save Aladdin, even if, by begging.
But Jafar had already put him in jail
Where nobody could hear him wail.

When the king found out, he said,
'This boy, I hope you did not behead.'
Jafar lied and said, 'Unfortunately, Yes.
Your royal and forgiving highness!'

Jasmine cried and felt extremely sad,
While Jafar was really happy and glad.
He needed Aladdin for his thieving job,
The magic cave, he wanted Aladdin to rob.

Jafar, finally could execute his grand plan,
He only had to convince the young man.
So Jafar dressed as a prisoner, so old,
About a magic treasure cave, he told.

'Would you like to own many bags of gold?
Then you must fetch them, I am too old.
Just get me the lamp from this cave,
You clever boy! So young and brave.'

'You can keep all the gold and jewels,
As long as you follow all my rules.'
Aladdin was not very hard to convince;
He had always dreamt of being a prince.

Jafar said, 'I'll show you a way out.
Hurry, before the soldiers start to shout.'
Aladdin and Abu followed the old man,
And out of the prison walls they ran.

They walked until the cave came into sight.
This Cave of Doom gave them a fright.
'Don't touch anything except the lamp,'
Said Jafar, 'Go on, I have a leg cramp.'

So Aladdin entered cautiously inside,
Seeing all this gold, his eyes opened wide.
Suddenly, a carpet came flying from up ahead.
'I am the flying carpet of this cave,' it said.

It offered Aladdin and Abu a magnificent ride,
And they flew deeper and deeper inside,
Till they saw the lamp on a hill;
Their task they were about to fulfil.

'Do not touch anything, Abu,' Aladdin said,

'Or we could all end up buried and dead.

I'll go and fetch the lamp,' said Aladdin,

And then we will celebrate our great win.'

Abu suddenly saw a glittering jewel

And forgot all about the golden rule.

He grabbed the jewel, they fell into trouble,

For the cave started to collapse into rubble.

Grabbing the lamp, Aladdin screamed.

It was worse than what he had dreamed.

With the carpet's help, they tried to escape,

For they found themselves in a terrible scrape.

They were trapped in the cave filled with dust;

In the wrong person, they had put their trust.

With only the carpet, lamp and Abu,

What was Aladdin supposed to do?

From the lamp, he cleaned the dirt.

He wiped it nicely with his own shirt.

Something from the lamp came out,

Which was huge and rather stout.

'At last I can breathe and I am free,

After ten thousand years of misery.

Ah, what is your wish dear master,

Some jewels or a house of plaster?'

'Who are you?' Aladdin exclaimed.

'I am a majestic genie,' he explained.

'I will grant any three wishes to you,

Your carpet and your pet monkey, Abu.'

'I bet you can't get us out of here,'
Said Aladdin to the genie without any fear.
The genie then pompously clapped his hands,
And they landed outside in the desert sands.

It was a desolate and extremely lonely place.
'See, I did it,' the genie said making a face.
'Now, about those three wishes,' Aladdin exclaimed.
'I am hearing you all wrong,' the genie proclaimed.

'You have only two wishes to spare,'
The powerful genie then did declare.
Aladdin firmly said, 'I didn't ask for that wish,'
'No more tricks,' said the genie, feeling foolish.

'I want to marry princess Jasmine!'
Said Aladdin with a silly looking grin.
'Apologies. I can't create love for you,
Master, this is the one thing I can't do.'

'I wish to be a prince with riches and might.'
Said Aladdin, imagining a future so bright.
'If you do this, genie, and fulfil my quest,
I will set you free as my third request.'

The genie gasped and couldn't believe his luck.
And while Abu looked on in awe, thunderstruck,
Aladdin became the royal prince of a distant land,
Boasting of a huge army and a palace so grand.

Meanwhile, Jafar told his parrot, perched on a tree,
'I thought he would surely bring the lamp to me.'
'Why don't you try to marry Princess Jasmine?'
Replied the parrot while Jafar rubbed his chin.

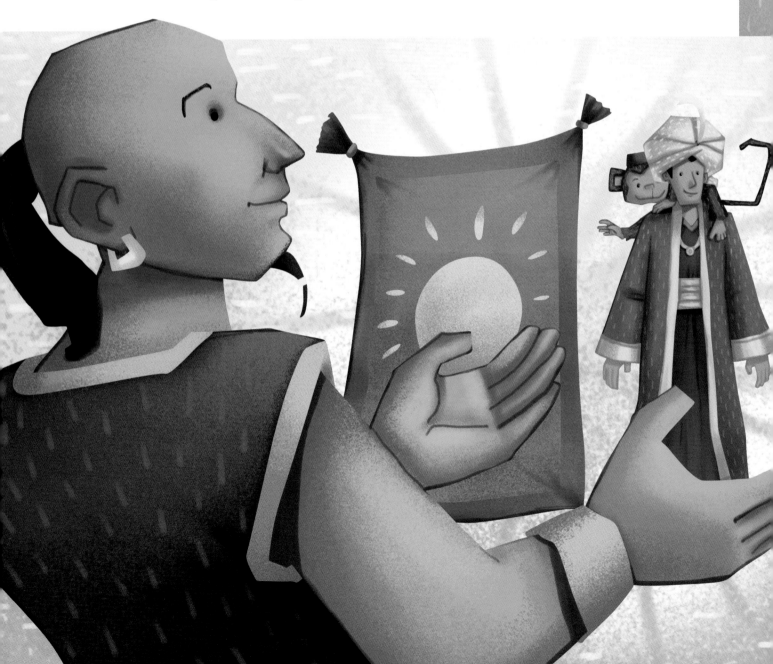

'Jasmine and the king you must delude.'

'Then kill them both,' the parrot continued.

After thinking on it for a long while,

Jafar stared and smiled a wicked smile.

He went to the king with an ancient book,

And said, 'Majesty, come and take a look.

I found this in the palace archives,

It will surely change all our lives.'

'If a prince, the princess does not choose
The advisor must walk into the king's shoes.
That means I must be the next new king,'
Declared Jafar, known by all to be cunning.

'Not possible,' said the king with a frown.
'How can an advisor inherit the crown?'
Jafar quickly waved his tall, magic stick,
And performed a mind-controlling trick!

The king was now in Jafar's control,
Jafar was about to achieve his goal.
Just then a guard entered and said at length,
'A new prince is in town with all his strength.'

Aladdin was elegantly dressed as royalty;

To Jasmine, he wanted to prove his loyalty.

But when Jasmine met Aladdin again,

She gave him a look of utter disdain.

'I will never marry you stranger,' she said.

She loved Aladdin and thought him dead.

The prince offered her a magic carpet ride;

Jasmine wanted to go but could not decide.

She finally agreed, they soared to the skies,

Flying high, Aladdin, she finally did recognise.

Jasmine was happy to find her love alive,

She wanted to marry him and be his wife.

Now the king knew they loved each other,
And she would not agree to marry another.
For his second wish, Aladdin asked for gold
And jewels for the princess to behold.

'As you wish,' said the genie grinning.
It was time for his fresh, new beginning.
'Aladdin, will you really now, set me free?
Remember, on this we did sincerely agree.'

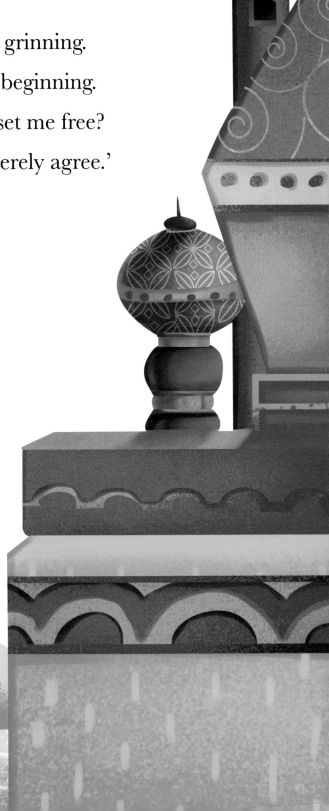
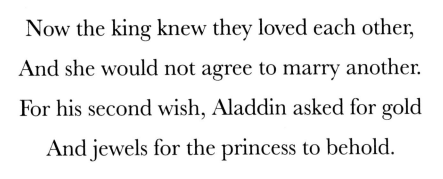

'I am sorry Genie, but I need you around.
Wait till I marry Jasmine and I am crowned.'
The genie then retired into his lamp,
Feeling disappointed, down and damp.

Jafar's parrot saw the lamp and swiped it.

He gave it to Jafar who rubbed and wiped it.

The genie appeared and got a scare,

How would he serve someone so unfair?

'The first wish I want is, to be king,'

Said Jafar who wanted everything.

Soon everybody was under Jafar's rule.

As a king, he was evil and cruel.

Jafar exposed Aladdin as a street rat,

And said Jasmine was just a spoiled brat.

Aladdin wanted to overthrow evil Jafar,

And send him to a place very far.

So he taunted Jafar and said,

'The princess you will never wed.

You are nothing but a foolish king,

And you can magically do nothing!'

Jafar shouted at the genie from his tower,

'Turn me into a sorcerer with immense power.'

The genie obliged and obeyed his command;

Jafar was now left with only one demand.

He asked Jasmine to marry him.

'Never,' said Jasmine, looking grim.

Jafar then put Jasmine in a cage.

'How dare you!' said Aladdin in a rage.

Then a brilliant idea came into Aladdin's mind.

'Jafar, you are not so powerful, you will find.

Only a genie, that much power can possess.'

What is he doing? wondered the genie in distress.

Jafar looked at the genie and said in heat,
'Turn me into a genie that no one can defeat.'
'As you wish master,' said the genie in surprise,
And Aladdin's grand plan, he did, then realise.

Suddenly Jafar, in the lamp, was trapped.
It was a tiny little place, so very cramped.
For Jafar had forgotten the genie rule,
In his haste, he had been made a fool.

A genie to a lamp, must be bound.

He cannot ever roam freely around.

A genie can only live to forever serve,

This was what evil Jafar did deserve.

Aladdin loved Jasmine and wanted to marry her,

But he had to be a prince for them to be together.

Aladdin looked at the genie for his last request,

He was sure that the genie would fulfil his quest.

Yet Aladdin kept his promise and set the genie free,

Even though Jasmine was sad and did not at all agree.

The king realised his daughter's pain and announced,

'I am not bound by any old traditions,' he pronounced.

'The princess from this day, can marry whoever she desires.

I will give to Aladdin my blessings and all that he requires.'

Jasmine and Aladdin married in joy and laughter,

And they lived happily ever after!